To my mother and loving mothers everywhere —K.D.

In memory of my mum —G.T.

Text copyright © 2015 by Kathy Duval
Jacket art and interior illustrations copyright © 2015 by Gerry Turley

All rights reserved. Published in the United States by Schwartz & Wade Books,
an imprint of Random House Children's Books, a division of Random House LLC,
a Penguin Random House Company, New York.

Schwartz & Wade Books and the colophon are trademarks of Random House LLC.

Visit us on the Web! randomhousekids.com

Educators and librarians, for a variety of teaching tools, visit us at RHTeachersLibrarians.com

Library of Congress Cataloging-in-Publication Data
Duval, Kathy.
A bear's year / Kathy Duval ; Gerry Turley.—First edition.
pages cm
Summary: Illustrations and simple, rhyming text describe a year in the lives of bears as they journey
through the seasons and raise their young.
ISBN 978-0-385-37011-0 (hc) — ISBN 978-0-385-37012-7 (glb) — ISBN 978-0-385-37013-4 (ebook)
[1. Stories in rhyme. 2. Bears—Fiction. 3. Seasons—Fiction.] I. Turley, Gerry, illustrator. II. Title.
PZ8.3.D946Be 2014
[E]—dc23
2013007900

The text of this book is set in Belen.
The illustrations were rendered using drawing and screen printing, which were then pieced together digitally.
Book design by Rachael Cole
MANUFACTURED IN CHINA
1 3 5 7 9 10 8 6 4 2

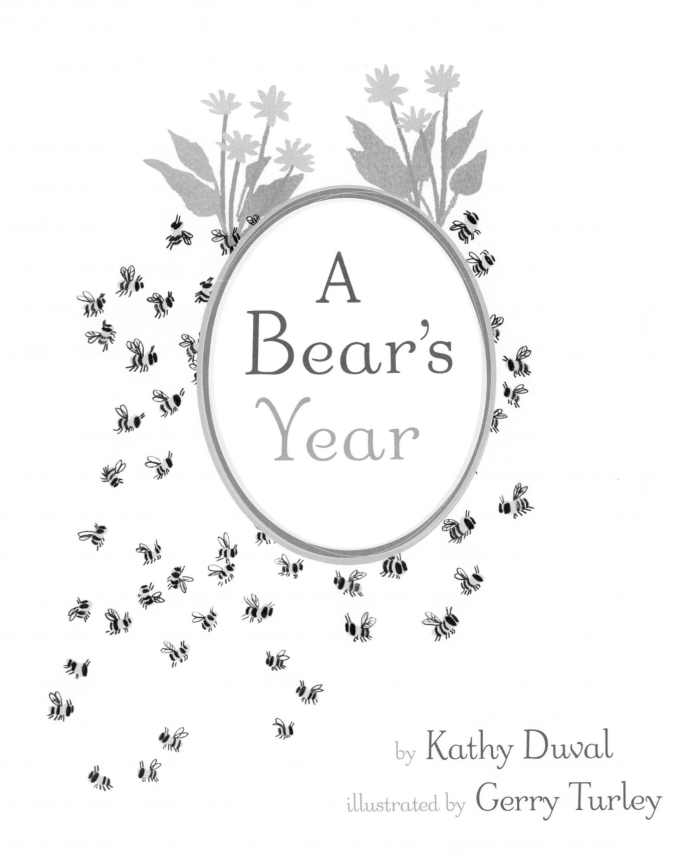

A Bear's Year

by Kathy Duval

illustrated by Gerry Turley

schwartz & wade books • new york

W inter Bear

drifts into sleep,

Earth's snowflake blanket

soft and deep.

Northern Lights

paint the sky.

Gray wolf wails

a lullaby.

A cozy dreamer

in her lair

cuddles newborn

baby bears.

Springtime Bear

wakes at last;

her springtime cubs

are growing fast.

They walk, then run

and climb so high

while Mama keeps

her watch nearby.

Cubs wrestle, tumble,

chase and hide—

then take a nap

side by side.

Summer Bear

treats her cubs

to juicy berries,

tasty grubs.

Cubs catch fish,

find bees that swarm,

and dig for roots

when days are warm.

For they must learn

what Mama knows

while flowers bloom

and grass still grows.

Autumn Bear

digs a den,

a sheltered bed

for this year's end.

Coats grow thick,

bodies strong.

Soon bears will doze

all winter long.

Food grows scarce.

Leaves turn gold.

Mountain's breath

will soon blow cold.

Days are short.

Nights are long.

North winds sing

winter's song.

Last year's cubs,

almost grown,

dream they'll soon

be on their own.

First snow falls.

Bears stay warm,

nestled close

in Earth's safe arms.

Winds subside.

Still descends.

Bears will sleep

till winter's end.